2-in-1 Junior Novel

Adapted by Catherine Hapka

Based on the character "Air Bud" created by Kevin DiCicco

Based on characters created by Paul Tamasy & Aaron Mendelsohn

The Legend of Santa Paws is based on the screenplay written by Robert Vince and Anna McRoberts

The Search for Santa Paws is based on the screenplay written by Robert Vince and Anna McRoberts

Disney PRESS

New York

Printed in the United States of America
First Edition
1 3 5 7 9 10 8 6 4 2
J689-1817-1-10196
Library of Congress Control Number on file.
ISBN 978-1-4231-3772-6
For more Disney Press fun, visit www.disneybooks.com

Part One

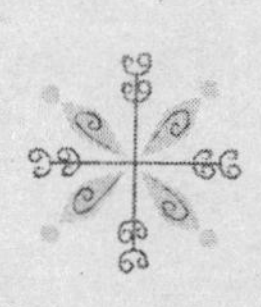

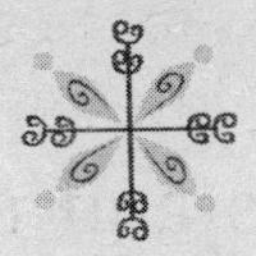

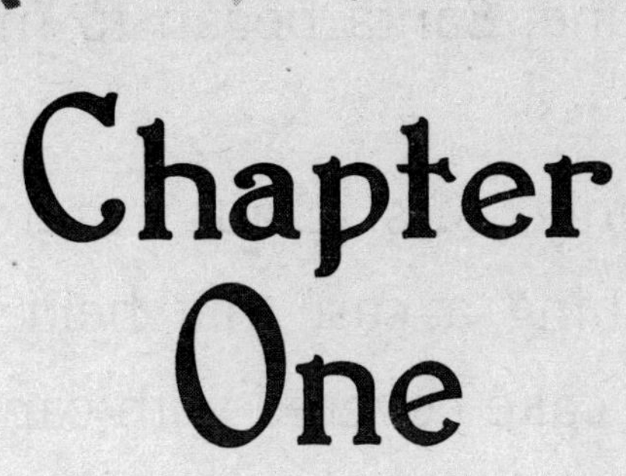

Chapter One

All boys and girls know about Santa Claus. But not many know the tale of Santa Paws. . . .

It was a few weeks before Christmas, and the elves and elf dogs in Santa's workshop were very busy. They were making toys for children all over the world. When Santa Claus walked in, the elves and elf dogs were singing a happy tune. Santa began to make his rounds.

Suddenly, Mrs. Claus entered. She was pushing a cart that held a large birthday cake covered with candles.

"Happy birthday, Santa, dear!" she called out.

"Special delivery, Santa," Eli the elf said. Eli was holding a large gift.

Eddy the elf dog was following him, carrying a letter in his mouth. "Just arrived by North Pole Express," he said.

Eddy was the head of the elf dogs. Along with the elves, they helped Santa with all his North Pole duties. Thanks to the magic of the Great Christmas Icicle, the elf dogs could talk. Of course, they could only be understood by those who believed in the magic of the holiday.

"A gift for me?" Santa exclaimed, taking the letter.

"From the Big Apple," Eli replied.

Santa's jolly expression faded as he read the letter. It turned out that his friend Mr. Hucklebuckle had passed away. The present had been sent by his lawyer, and it was Mr. Hucklebuckle's last gift for Santa.

Santa unwrapped the box. Inside was a fluffy white toy puppy. It had a red ribbon around its neck. A tag stamped with the Hucklebuckle Toys logo—an outline of a puppy—hung from the ribbon.

Santa sighed and shook his head sadly. "Mr. Hucklebuckle was a great ambassador for the Santa cause."

After that, Santa didn't seem quite the same to his family and friends. His Christmas spirit seemed forced.

Mrs. Claus and Eli were worried about Santa. So they thought of a plan to cheer him up.

Santa walked into an ice cave near his workshop. The Great Christmas Icicle hung inside. The sparkling Icicle was the source of all the magic in the North Pole. It provided Santa with his magical powers. He wore a chunk of the crystal on a chain around his neck.

"Eli, what was so important?" Santa asked, looking around.

Eli was holding the toy puppy. Mrs. Claus and Eddy were there, too.

"You've been feeling a little blue," Eli said. "With the help of a little Christmas magic, we can cheer you up."

Eddy had a red-and-white striped dog collar in his mouth. Hanging from it was a tiny chunk of the Icicle. It was magical, just like the one Santa wore around his neck. Eli buckled the collar onto the stuffed puppy.

The Great Christmas Icicle began to

glow. Magic dust swirled through the air and surrounded the crystal on the collar. The toy's eyes sparkled. . . .

Woof! The toy became a real, live puppy!

Santa was amazed. He put out his hand and shook the puppy's paw. "I'm going to name you Paws," he said. "You and I are going to be best friends for all eternity!"

"Eternity?" Paws asked. "How long is that?" The magic from the Great Christmas Icicle had also given Paws the power to speak.

"Ho, ho, ho! Why, forever, young pup!" Santa replied.

Santa still missed Mr. Hucklebuckle,

of course. But his new companion would remind him of the joys of friendship. This helped Santa get over his sadness, just as Eli had hoped it would. From that moment on, Santa and Paws were the best of buddies.

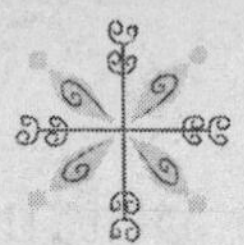

Chapter Two

Far from the North Pole, in the heart of New York City, James and Kate Huckle stood in front of a beautiful old building. The young married couple was a long way from their home in Los Angeles. They looked at a sign out front that read, HUCKLEBUCKLE TOYS: PURVEYOR OF TOYS, MAKER OF JOYS.

"Look at this place," Mrs. Huckle exclaimed as they entered a huge room filled with old-fashioned toys. "It's so nostalgic."

"Yeah, that's one word for it." Mr. Huckle made a face. The place was dusty and coated with cobwebs.

Mrs. Huckle pulled a cover off a piece of furniture. "Is this a Santa chair?" she asked, touching the red velvet seat.

Mr. Huckle nodded. "Grandpa used to dress up for the kids. I'm sure the suit is still around here somewhere. He loved the whole Christmas season."

An older gentleman walked in, leaning on a cane. "Mr. Hucklebuckle, I presume," he said. "I'm Mr. Stewart."

"Actually, it's Huckle," Mr. Huckle said. "I changed it years ago."

Mr. Stewart was Mr. Hucklebuckle's lawyer. He explained to Mr. Huckle that his grandfather had left the store to him.

"We're going to put the building on the market immediately," Mr. Huckle told Mr. Stewart.

"There is, however, one stipulation," Mr. Stewart told the couple. "You need to operate the store through one Christmas season profitably before the deed can be transferred."

"But we live in Los Angeles!" Mr. Huckle complained. "Besides, kids don't want to play with this stuff anymore. It's old-fashioned."

Mr. Stewart smiled. "Your grandfather used to say that children's imaginations don't change."

"We'll keep the store open through Christmas, Mr. Stewart," Mrs. Huckle promised. She could see the store had been wonderful once, the kind of place she would have loved when she was little. Running the grand old store would be a nice way to spend the season.

Mr. Stewart told them they could stay in Mr. Hucklebuckle's apartment on the top floor of the building. "There's plenty of room," he added. "I'm sure your children will love it here."

Mr. and Mrs. Huckle traded a sad

look. "We haven't been blessed with any children," Mrs. Huckle said.

Mr. Stewart changed the subject. He handed over some paperwork, then left.

When he was gone, the Huckles settled in. There was a lot to do to get the toy store ready in time for the holiday season.

The Huckles got right to work putting Hucklebuckle Toys back in business. Mrs. Huckle cleaned and polished the old walls and shelves until they shone. The toys became bright and colorful again as she wiped off the dust.

Mr. Huckle looked over the paper-work. He wasn't happy about what he saw. "This store has barely broken even for the past thirty years," he complained. "We need something to bring in customers."

"What about a store Santa?" his wife suggested. The beautiful old chair they had seen before would be perfect for Santa Claus to sit in while he listened to children's Christmas wishes.

"That's a great idea!" Mr. Huckle exclaimed. Then he frowned. "Where do you get a store Santa?"

"I don't know," Mrs. Huckle said. "The Internet?"

Mr. Huckle nodded and reached for his laptop. He was sure Santa was just a few clicks away.

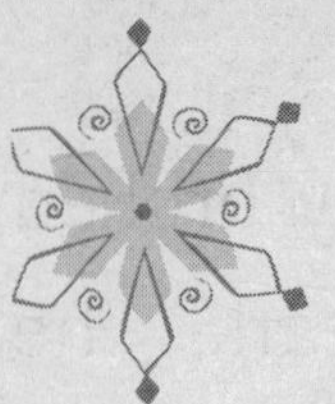
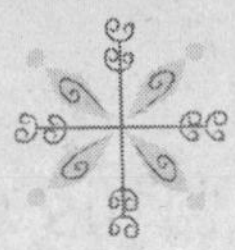
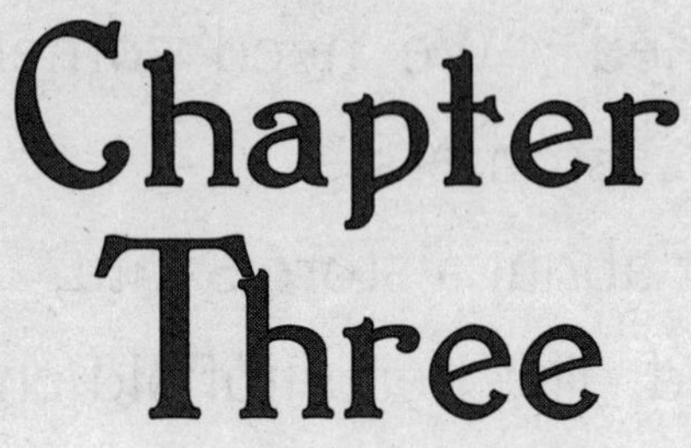

Chapter Three

Outside Hucklebuckle Toys, a ten-year-old girl peered through the store's front window. Her name was Willamina, but everyone called her Will. She stared dreamily at a bright red bicycle in a display. But when Mrs. Huckle went to clean the window, Will rushed away. She wasn't supposed to be there, and she didn't want anyone to notice her.

Will headed for the Sixty-fourth Street Home for Girls. It was a rundown old building where girls like Will lived. Girls with no families of their own.

While Will was walking toward the back door, a new girl was arriving at the front one. Her name was Quinn, and she was five years old. She clung tightly to the hand of a social worker named Mrs. Gibson.

"Don't worry, Quinn," Mrs. Gibson said. "There will be other kids for you to play with."

Mrs. Gibson rang the bell. A woman yanked open the door.

"Yes?" she said impatiently.

"Ms. Stout?" Mrs. Gibson said. "I believe you're expecting us. This is Quinn."

"Oh, yes, the new one," Ms. Stout said, barely glancing at Quinn. "Come right in."

The building was even gloomier inside than it was outside. "This place could use a little Christmas cheer," Mrs. Gibson said.

"If I got more money from the state maybe I could afford some Christmas decorations," Ms. Stout said, sounding annoyed. She held out her hand.

Mrs. Gibson handed her a check. "For Quinn's monthly care," she said.

Ms. Stout peeked at the check, then walked Mrs. Gibson out. When the social worker had gone, Ms. Stout pointed to an old bench.

"Sit there," she ordered Quinn. "I'll have someone show you around and, more importantly, fill you in on all my rules." She turned away. "Willamina!" she shouted.

Will was still outside when she heard Ms. Stout shouting her name, sounding angry and impatient. That was no surprise. Ms. Stout almost always sounded that way.

Will put on a burst of speed, but she wasn't fast enough. Ms. Stout caught her trying to sneak in a back window.

"Where have you been?" Ms. Stout snarled.

She ordered Will to show Quinn around and tell her the rules. "New kid. Much cuter than you—and younger. I'm sure she'll go fast." Will was annoyed. Just because she was the oldest, Ms. Stout made her do everything! Will started showing Quinn around.

"This is the living room," she said.

"Where's the Christmas tree?" Quinn asked.

"Ms. Stout can't stand Christmas, so none of us are allowed to have it." Then Will introduced some other girls who were cleaning the room. "That's Janie, Meg, Taylor, and Mary."

"What happened to your parents?" Janie asked Quinn.

"They didn't make it," Quinn said sadly. "They had to go to heaven."

"Mine neither," Taylor said. "Janie's, too, but she still thinks they're going to come for her."

"They *are*," Janie insisted. "You'll see."

"Nobody's parents are coming," Will said. "That's why we're here. Your only chance is to get adopted."

"What's ''dopted'?" Quinn asked.

"*A*-dopted," Will corrected. "It's when a new mom and dad think you're cute and take you home. They like little kids. Not older ones like me. Come on, I'll show you where we sleep."

She turned and hurried away without waiting for a reply. What good would it do her to stand around talking about getting adopted? Sure, that might happen for some of the younger, cuter girls, such as Quinn. But Will was a realist. It was way too late for her. She knew better than to get her hopes up.

Chapter Four

In the North Pole, someone else was worried, too—Santa Claus. As Christmas Eve drew closer, he was busy reading all the letters from children around the world. It seemed to Santa that something had gone wrong with the spirit of the holiday.

In order to remind everyone what

Christmas was truly about, Santa and Paws were going on a quick trip south. Santa thought New York would be the perfect place to start because there they could celebrate the memory of Mr. Hucklebuckle.

"We'll visit some ambassadors for the Santa cause, talk to the children, and be back in a Christmas minute," Santa said as he walked to his sleigh. He was wearing a red flannel shirt, reddish brown corduroys, and a warm wool overcoat.

Eli, Eddy the elf dog, and Mrs. Claus were there to see off Santa and Paws.

Mrs. Claus handed Santa a small suitcase. "You seem to have forgotten your North Pole pin." She took a pin from her pocket and attached it to Santa's suspenders.

Santa kissed her on the cheek and waved to all the elves. Soon the sleigh and reindeer rose into the air. Santa and Paws were on their way to the Big Apple.

A short while later, Santa landed his sleigh in Central Park. He climbed out of the sleigh with Paws right behind him. He grabbed the suitcase that held his Santa suit, just in case he needed it.

"Okay, fellas, you get some rest," he told the reindeer. "Come on, Paws."

Then Santa led the way out of the

park. He and Paws stopped at the edge of a busy street filled with honking taxis. Dozens of pedestrians rushed by from every direction. It was like nothing Paws had ever seen before.

"This is way huger than the workshop!" the puppy exclaimed as he looked around.

"Now, Paws," Santa said, "only those who believe in the magic of Christmas can understand North Pole animals like you. So you need to be very careful."

Then a woman bumped into Santa. Her packages went flying, and her hat rolled into the street. It was Ms. Stout.

"Watch where you're going!" she complained.

"She's not very jolly," commented Paws.

Ms. Stout gathered up her packages and rushed away.

Santa watched her go, feeling a little sad. It was obvious that she hadn't understood Paws. All she'd heard was barking. That meant she didn't believe in the magic of Christmas. How many people were just like her? That was what he was here to find out.

Then Santa noticed Ms. Stout's hat in the street.

"I'll get it!" Paws said. He ran out to grab it.

Santa saw a cab rushing toward the puppy. "Paws, no!" he cried.

He jumped forward and pushed Paws out of the way. The cab swerved, but not fast enough. Santa was knocked to the ground and hit his head.

"Santa's hurt!" Paws cried out in a panic. "Someone help!"

But the people around him only heard barking. Paws rushed down the street, trying to get someone—anyone—to understand.

Meanwhile, the cab driver had tried to find someone who knew first aid. The only one to step forward was a man named Gus.

Unfortunately, Gus was lying. He only wanted to rob Santa. He convinced the cabbie and the other onlookers to leave, then grabbed Santa's suitcase. He took the crystal that hung from Santa's neck.

Just then Santa moaned.

"You all right there, bud?" Gus said. "I saved your life."

"Where am I?" Santa mumbled.

"New York City," Gus told him. "Ring a bell?"

"All I hear is bells." Santa sat up and rubbed his head. "Jingle bells. Any way you could direct me to . . . *uhh* . . ." Santa couldn't remember where he had been going.

Gus noticed a police officer strolling down the block. "I'm in a bit of a hurry, bud," he said. "See you around."

Gus took off with the suitcase.

Santa barely noticed. He couldn't remember who or where he was. In fact, he couldn't remember much of anything at all!

"Bud . . . ?" he mumbled uncertainly.

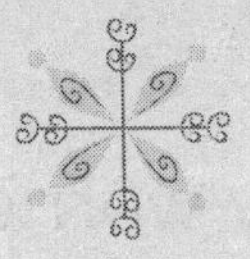

Chapter Five

Paws ran up and down the streets of New York, hoping to find someone who could understand him and help Santa. But nobody understood him. Finally he ran back to the scene of the accident. By then, Santa was gone!

Now Paws *really* didn't know what to do. He began to search the area. Paws was very worried. What had become of Santa Claus?

Gus wasn't worried about Santa at all. He hurried off carrying all the things he'd stolen from Santa.

Soon Gus headed back to the park bench where he spent most of his time. He looked at Santa's crystal but wasn't sure what it was. So Gus decided to wear the crystal around his own neck. He opened Santa's suitcase, hoping something valuable was inside. All he found was Santa's suit, hat, and gloves.

At first Gus was upset. Then he noticed a man nearby. He was dressed in a Santa suit and ringing a bell. People kept dropping money into his bucket.

So Gus put on Santa's suit and chased the other Santa away. Then Gus picked up the bell and opened the suitcase, placing it at his feet.

"Ho, ho, ho!" he called out, ringing the bell.

Within seconds, someone dropped a few coins into the suitcase!

Gus smiled. He hadn't found cash in the suitcase, but this was even better. He could use the Santa suit to trick people into giving him money. They would think they were being kind and donating to charity. But he would keep it all for himself.

"Happy Christmas to ya," he called out, ringing the bell even louder.

Back at Hucklebuckle Toys, Mr. Huckle was worried. "The lady at the Santa Claus agency laughed at me when I asked if they had any available store Santas," he told his wife.

Mrs. Huckle barely heard him. She was staring at the results of all her cleaning. "I had no idea how beautiful this store was," she said.

"Don't get too attached to this place," her husband reminded her. "It'll be up for sale as soon as it's ours."

"It was kind of nice to have an extra project," she said. "I was dreading the

Christmas season without a child."

That made Mr. Huckle forget about everything else for a moment. He hugged her, knowing exactly how she felt. Both of them wished for children of their own. "Let's call it a night."

He wasn't sure which switches worked with which lights. So he just flipped them all as he headed upstairs.

Across the street, the real Santa sat on a bench. He'd wandered around for hours hoping to remember who he was and where he was supposed to be going. But he still had no idea, so he'd stopped for a rest. He blinked as the Hucklebuckle Toys sign suddenly lit up.

"Hucklebuckle Toys," he murmured.

Why did that name seem so familiar? He squinted at the puppy logo.

A second later the sign switched off again. Santa's memory faded just as quickly. He yawned, feeling very tired. Maybe going into that toy store would help him remember something. But that would have to wait until the morning. With another yawn, he curled up on the bench and went to sleep.

Chapter Six

The next day, Mr. Huckle looked up as the bell chimed above the door of Hucklebuckle Toys. An older, jolly-looking man with a round belly and a full white beard walked in.

"Hey, the agency must have found one!" Mr. Huckle exclaimed. "Can you start today?"

The man was Santa, though he still hadn't regained his memory. He stared at Mr. Huckle, feeling very confused.

"Start?" he echoed.

"You're looking for work, right?" Mrs. Huckle asked with a smile.

Santa thought for a second. Was he looking for work? He had no idea. "More like a home, really," he said. "I'm new in town and a little disoriented."

"I didn't get your name," Mr. Huckle said.

Santa had to stop and think about that, too. "Bud," he said after a moment, remembering what Gus had called him. "They call me Bud."

The Huckles were puzzled when

he asked what kind of work they wanted him to do.

"In-store Santa," Mrs. Huckle explained. "You talk to the kids, you ask them what they want for Christmas. . . ."

"That sounds like something I could handle," Santa agreed.

"We do have a spare room," Mrs. Huckle offered.

Santa accepted. He smiled as he followed Mr. and Mrs. Huckle toward the back of the store.

It was another dreary winter day at the Sixty-fourth Street Home for Girls. Will watched through an upstairs window as Ms. Stout stepped out the front door. The woman paused just long enough to flirt with Franklin, the local dogcatcher, who happened to be passing by. Then she disappeared around the corner, heading toward the beauty shop.

Will turned away from the window to find Quinn watching her.

"Where are you going?" Quinn asked.

"Who says I'm going anywhere?" Will replied.

Quinn looked at the gloves in Will's hands. "Can I come?" Quinn asked.

Will shrugged. She sort of liked the new kid.

"Okay," she said, "but we have to hurry." She grabbed her coat. "Ms. Stout takes two hours to get her hair done."

❄ ❄ ❄

Over at the toy store, Mr. and Mrs. Huckle were helping Santa settle in. They had given him Mr. Hucklebuckle's old Santa outfit.

"I hope your grandpa's suit fits Bud," Mrs. Huckle said to her husband.

"Grandpa Hucklebuckle used to say that Santa himself gave it to him," Mr. Huckle said.

Santa walked back in wearing the suit. The Huckles stared at him.

"You look great," Mr. Huckle said. "If I wasn't an adult I'd believe you were Santa himself!"

"I don't think you're ever too old to believe," Santa said with a smile.

Soon Santa was seated near the front of the store in the large red velvet chair, waiting for children to arrive.

Outside, Will and Quinn were staring in the window at the red bicycle in the display. They had walked around for a while before ending up in front of Hucklebuckle Toys.

"Isn't that the most beautiful bike you've ever seen?" Will said.

Quinn couldn't stop looking at all the toys. "Is this Santa's workshop?" she wondered aloud.

"No, it's just a toy store," Will said.

At that moment, Quinn spotted Santa through the window. She gasped and ran toward the door. Then she stopped, hesitating. Mrs. Huckle noticed the little girl and invited her in.

"I don't got any money to buy toys," Quinn said.

"That's okay," Mrs. Huckle replied. "Would you like to see Santa?"

She brought the girls inside. Quinn climbed onto Santa's lap. Will stood off to the side, watching.

"What would you like Santa to get you for Christmas?" Santa asked Quinn.

"I'd like it if you could give Will that bike in the window. She's really nice, even if she doesn't believe in Santa," Quinn said. "And the girls at the foster home need something to cheer them up, like a puppy or something."

Just then the store clock chimed loudly. Will glanced at it in a panic. "Come on, Quinn," she called. "We have to go!"

"Well, we'll see what Santa can do," Santa Claus said.

The two girls bolted out of the store. They had to get back to the home before Ms. Stout returned from the beauty salon.

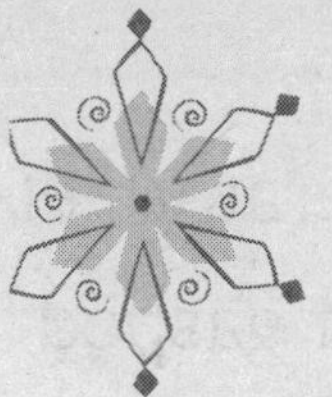

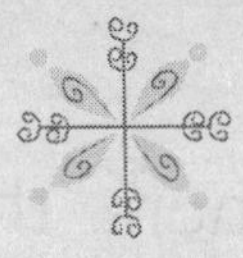

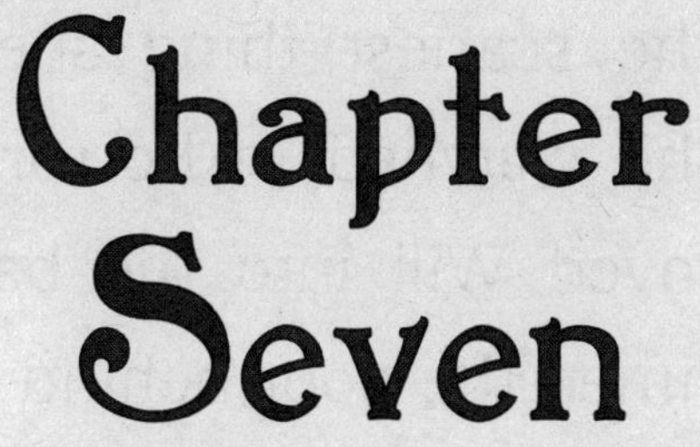

Chapter Seven

Will and Quinn ran as fast as they could. But Ms. Stout caught them trying to sneak in. She blamed Will for everything, as usual, and made her go to the basement.

"When you break the rules, you get to spend all night down here in the basement," Ms. Stout scolded.

Just then, the trash incinerator let out a growl and a hiss. Quinn gasped. It was the scariest thing she'd ever heard! She watched in horror as Ms. Stout shoved Will into the basement and slammed the door behind her.

In another part of New York, a Scottish terrier named Haggis was waiting on the sidewalk outside a deli.

"Hurry up," he called through the open door.

Just then, Paws came around the corner. He'd been searching all night and still hadn't found Santa. He'd gone so far that he couldn't even remember the way back to the sleigh.

As Paws watched, two dogs ran out of the deli carrying meat. One was a bulldog named T-Money. The other was Rasta, a puli with Jamaican-style dreadlocks.

The deli owner rushed out after them. "Get out of here!" he shouted angrily.

"Maybe those dogs have seen Santa," Paws wondered aloud.

Just then the dogcatcher's truck arrived.

Haggis and his friends ran away. Paws followed them down an alley.

"Allow me to introduce myself," he said. "I'm Paws, Santa Claus's dog, from the North Pole."

"Yeah, *mon*," Rasta said. "And I be the tooth fairy!"

None of the dogs believed Paws. When he asked for their help finding Santa, they just laughed. But the dogs stopped laughing when Franklin the dogcatcher sneaked up and threw his net over them! Then he swooped a leash attached to a long pole around Paws' neck.

"Gotcha!" Franklin shouted.

Paws' collar glowed; a second later the dog walked right through the leash and ran away. The magic crystal on his collar had protected him. Paws was surprised but glad he had escaped.

Franklin was confused, but he didn't

worry about it too much. At least he'd caught the other three dogs.

"Help us, *mon*!" Rasta called to Paws.

The pup followed the dogcatcher's truck as it drove away.

A short while later, Franklin parked his truck at the dog pound.

"All right, doggies," he said, "let's get you in lockup."

He heard barking behind him. It was that white puppy who had escaped earlier! Franklin chased after him.

Paws had come back to help the other dogs. Even though they had caused trouble before, Paws didn't believe *any* dog deserved to go to the pound.

Paws circled around Franklin and used his magic crystal to open the back of the truck.

"Come on, guys!" Paws cried.

The three dogs jumped out. Franklin ran around the truck just in time to see them escape.

The dogs ran into an alley. They were sorry they'd doubted Paws.

"Now we're your peeps," T-Money said. "We'll keep an eye out for Santa."

"Thanks," Paws said.

Just then Franklin caught up with them. The street dogs distracted him long enough for Paws to get away.

Paws was disappointed he and the

other dogs had been separated again. He was sure they would meet up later, though. He was glad to have some new friends. But he still didn't know where to go. "How am I ever going to find Santa?" he said, worried.

He wandered through the darkening streets. "Santa?" he called. "Where are you?" It sounded like howling to most people, but one person understood him.

Quinn had been looking out the window of the home and heard Paws. She climbed down the fire escape to the street. "I've never met a dog who talks before."

"I came from the North Pole," Paws told her. "My name's Paws."

"I'm Quinn. Does that mean you know Santa Claus?"

"He's my best friend," Paws said.

Through the window, Quinn heard Ms. Stout yelling about the barking. "I have to go," she told Paws.

"Can I come with you?" Paws asked. "I'm really lost."

"The lady here is mean," Quinn warned. "So we have to hide you real good."

Then she and Paws snuck into the girls' home together.

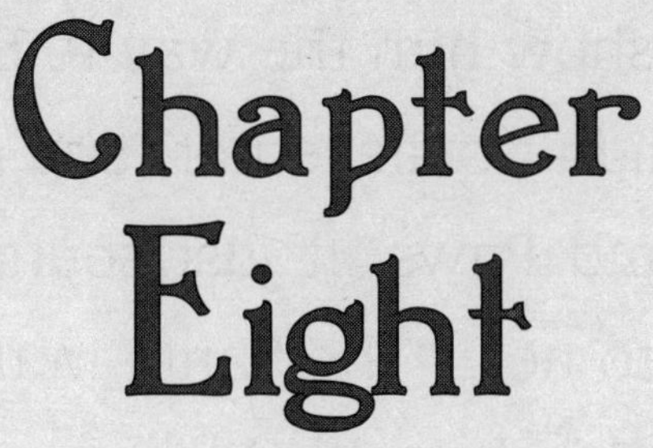

Chapter Eight

The next morning at the home, Will was on her way to breakfast when she heard barking. It was coming from the supply closet. She looked in and saw Quinn and Paws—and a lot of Christmas lights and decorations!

"What are you doing in here?" Will asked. "Where did you find this puppy?"

"He came from the North Pole on Santa's sleigh," Quinn explained. "We need to show him the way to Santa."

Will didn't believe her. She couldn't understand Paws. It just sounded like barking to her. "The Santa in the store is not real," she told Quinn.

Still, she thought Paws was cute and helped hide him from Ms. Stout.

That same day, customers poured into Hucklebuckle Toys. Children were lined up out the door waiting to see Santa.

"Bud is so amazing," Mrs. Huckle told her husband. "The kids are just drawn to him."

The parents liked Santa, too. He

convinced bratty kids to behave and selfish kids to be generous. Plus, he put everyone in the Christmas spirit.

A TV news crew came to report about the crowds—and the special Santa.

"The kids really seem to love you," the TV reporter said. "With hundreds of toy store Santas all across New York City, what makes you so special?"

"I'm just an ambassador for the Santa cause," Santa said, "spreading the Christmas spirit to children around the world."

Mr. Huckle was thrilled. People were spending money at the toy store. If the store made a profit, he and his wife would have met Mr. Hucklebuckle's terms. That meant they would be able to sell the place and go back to LA—where they belonged.

At the North Pole, Mrs. Claus and Eli the head elf were worried. They hadn't heard from Santa since he'd left.

"Santa and Paws should be home by now," Mrs. Claus said, concerned.

"Let's check the map," Eli suggested.

Their magical tracker showed them that Santa was still in New York. So was Paws. But they weren't together!

"Santa would never leave Paws alone," Mrs. Claus exclaimed. "He's just a pup! Eddy, Eli, you need to go to New York and find them!"

Eli quickly began preparations for their trip. There was no time to lose.

After the newscast, even more children flocked to Hucklebuckle Toys to see Santa. They kept him busy from morning until night.

"I'm really worried about Bud," Mrs. Huckle told her husband.

Santa was really tired. Mr. Huckle took a turn in the Santa suit to help. But the kids didn't like him as much.

Worse yet, when Quinn and Paws went by the toy store to see if the Santa they had seen on the news was Paws' friend, they found Mr. Huckle wearing the suit instead.

"That's not the real Santa," Paws told Quinn.

Sadly, the pair walked to the girls' home. Paws knew he had to find Santa and get him back to the North Pole.

Quinn decided to let the other girls meet the puppy. "His name is Paws," she told them.

Then Paws popped out from under the blankets on Quinn's bed.

"I'm Santa Claus's best friend from the North Pole," he said.

"He just talked!" Janie cried.

The others heard it, too. Everyone except Will. She still only heard barking.

"Only kids who truly believe in Christmas spirit can hear me talk," Paws explained.

The others wanted Will to believe. So they started singing a cheerful song about believing in Christmas magic. Paws sang along, too.

"If you don't quiet that puppy, Ms. Stout is going to hear him barking!" Will said.

Sure enough, Ms. Stout stomped into the girls' room. "What is going on?" she demanded. "Willamina, who brought a puppy in here?"

Quinn tried to explain that she was the one who'd found Paws. But Ms. Stout blamed Will, as usual.

Then she spotted the crystal on Paws' collar. "That's a pretty gem," she said, yanking it off.

Ms. Stout scooped up Paws and locked him and Will in the basement. Then she chased Quinn back upstairs.

In the dark basement, Will sang a sad song. Then she began to cry. Paws tried to comfort her. At first Will didn't understand what he was saying. Then she wrapped her arms around the puppy and closed her eyes.

Finally, Will looked up, amazed. "I can understand you, Paws!"

The pair snuggled together, and the basement didn't seem quite so scary.

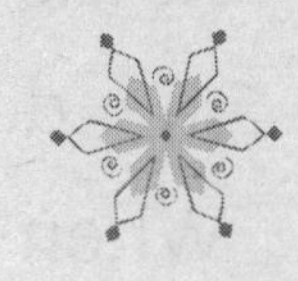

Chapter Nine

In the morning, things weren't going well at Hucklebuckle Toys. Santa was late, and children were already lined up to see him. When Mrs. Huckle went to his room, she found him looking weak and sick. Then Santa stumbled and collapsed!

"James, call an ambulance!" Mrs. Huckle cried.

❄ ❄ ❄

At the home, Ms. Stout called Franklin, the dogcatcher, to take Paws away. When they opened the basement door, they found Will sitting on the floor with a white toy puppy.

Franklin was confused. Ms. Stout was annoyed. Will was horrified.

Will didn't understand what had happened to Paws. She didn't know that without his magic crystal, Paws turned back into a toy! Only his eyes still showed the life inside him.

Ms. Stout didn't know, either, but she didn't care. Without Will seeing, she dropped the stuffed puppy onto the conveyor belt to the incinerator. It

Paws and Santa Claus did nearly everything together and soon became best buddies.

"Our landing spot is Central Park," Santa told Paws as they arrived in New York City.

"How am I ever going to find Santa?" Paws wondered as he searched the streets of New York.

T-Money, Rasta, and Haggis all offered to help Paws look for Santa Claus.

"What would you like Santa to get you for Christmas?" Santa Claus asked Quinn.

"You do believe in Christmas, after all," Paws told Will—and, suddenly, she could understand the puppy!

Everyone waved good-bye as Santa and Paws flew back to the North Pole.

"The Great Christmas Icicle brought me back. I'm Santa Paws now," the pup told the girls.

The Legend of Santa Paws

"Puppy Paws has to understand. He's the future of Christmas," his dad, Santa Paws, told Santa Claus and the elves.

The *Naughty* book showed a puppy named Budderball eating his family's turkey.

“Budderball! I finally found you!” Puppy Paws shouted as he tumbled out of the chimney.

“If he’s Santa Paws’ son, then why did he get me in *more* trouble?” Budderball asked the other Buddies.

"The Buddies and I flew that small sleigh to the North Pole," Puppy Paws said. "Maybe we can fly Santa's sleigh."

"Thank you, Buddies. You're the best friends I've ever had," Puppy Paws told them just before takeoff.

"This is the greatest Christmas ever!" Tiny told Puppy Paws and the Buddies when they arrived at his new home.

"Great work, pups!" Santa told the Buddies when he and Santa Paws arrived to pick up Puppy Paws.

would automatically turn on later that night, when it was time to burn the trash.

Eli and Eddy the elf dog were on their way to New York in an elf taxi. They followed the signal from a magical tracker to Central Park. It led them right to Gus, since he was wearing Santa's magic crystal.

Gus was amazed to see a real live elf and a talking dog. "Well, Gus," he told himself, "you have finally lost it."

"That's Santa's crystal!" Eli said. "Where did you get this?"

Gus told them about the taxi accident. He even admitted to robbing

Santa. "I feel terrible about it," he added.

He returned the crystal to Eli and Eddy. They knew Santa was in grave danger without it. The necklace helped Santa live forever—without it, he would become sick.

"We've got to find him before it's too late!" Eddy exclaimed.

Eli, Eddy, and Gus found the sleigh. The reindeer had stayed hidden in the park, waiting for Santa to return. They'd finished all their food a while ago and were weak with hunger.

"We need to find some eggnog, gingerbread cookies, fruitcake—things like that," Eli said.

Gus was ready to help. He rushed off to buy food for the reindeer with the money he'd collected playing Santa.

Eli and Eddy went to find Paws. They followed the tracker's signal to the Sixty-fourth Street Home for Girls.

Lucky for them, Ms. Stout was out on a date with Franklin. Eli and Eddy explained who they were to the girls.

"Thank goodness you're here!" Quinn cried.

The girls told Eli and Eddy what had happened to Paws, and how Ms. Stout had taken off his collar.

"His crystal!" Eli cried. He knew that Paws needed the magic from the crystal on his collar in order to be a real live puppy.

The girls didn't know what Ms. Stout had done with the collar—or with Paws.

"We have to put his crystal back on before his life force runs out," Eli said.

Will took charge. She offered to search Ms. Stout's room and assigned a different part of the house to each of the other girls. Paws had helped Will rediscover the magic of Christmas. She wanted to do whatever she could to save her new friend.

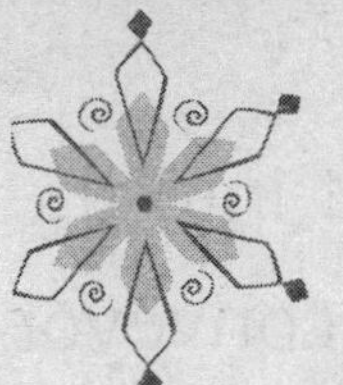

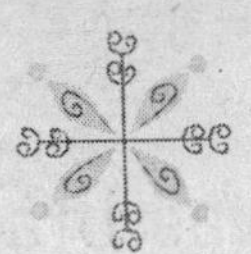

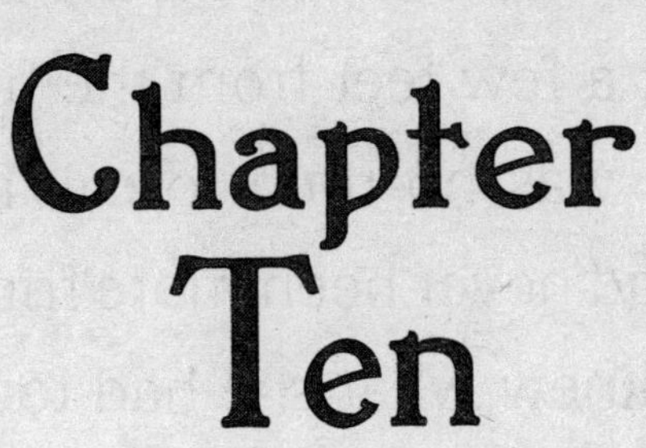

Chapter Ten

Quinn was passing the basement door when she heard the incinerator roar to life. It was time to burn the trash.

"Oh, my goodness!" Suddenly Quinn knew where Paws must be.

Quinn raced down the stairs. The basement was dark and terrifying. The incinerator was even scarier! But

Quinn was brave. She peered into the trash chute. Paws was on the conveyor belt, just a few feet from the fire.

There was no time to call for help. Quinn had never been more frightened, but she knew what she had to do.

"Hang on, Paws," she called. "I'm coming!"

Upstairs, the other girls had gathered in the living room. Will ran in. "I found the crystal," she called, holding up the collar. "But Paws wasn't there!"

Suddenly everyone heard a scream. It was coming from the basement!

Will ran downstairs. Eli and Eddy were right behind her.

"I have to save Paws!" shouted Quinn.

Paws was teetering right on the edge of the conveyor belt. Quinn grabbed him just in the nick of time. She crawled to safety and handed him to Eli.

"There's still life force in him." The elf reattached the crystal to Paws' collar.

The crystal glowed. A second later, Paws was a real puppy again!

"Good to see you, Paws," Eli said. "We have to find Santa. We have to get him his crystal back."

Meanwhile, Gus figured out Santa had been working at Hucklebuckle Toys. A boy named Jimmy had found Gus with the reindeer in Central Park. Jimmy was wearing a North Pole pin that Santa had given him at the toy store. Gus rushed to tell the others.

Gus, the elves, Paws, Quinn, and Will hurried to Hucklebuckle Toys.

"We're here to save Santa Claus," Quinn announced when Mr. Huckle came to the door.

"You mean Bud?" Mr. Huckle asked.

"Bud *is* Santa Claus," Will said.

Eddy the elf dog nodded. "Santa lost his magic crystal, and his health must have been deteriorating ever since."

"That dog is talking!" Mr. Huckle exclaimed.

"I see you believe in the Christmas spirit," Paws said.

"I didn't always." Then Mr. Huckle explained that Santa was in the hospital. "He's in critical condition."

Eli used North Pole magic to turn the elf taxi into an ambulance. Then they all rushed to the hospital. On the way, they came up with a plan.

At the hospital, the Huckles, Will, and Quinn sneaked Santa out on a gurney. Eli and Gus were waiting with the ambulance. They all got in and sped off.

Gus drove. Eli, Eddy, and Paws sat in back with Santa. They put his crystal around his neck. The crystal glowed faintly. There was no time to lose.

Chapter Eleven

Back at the girls' home, Ms. Stout had just arrived. But the door was locked. She shouted for Will to let her in.

When the front door opened, Mrs. Gibson was there. The social worker told Ms. Stout that a neighbor named Eli Elf had called. He reported that the children had been left alone all night and that two of them—Will and Quinn—were missing.

Ms. Stout tried to make up a story to explain, but it did no good.

"You are no longer permitted in this house," Mrs. Gibson told Ms. Stout. "By order of the state of New York."

Ms. Stout would no longer be in charge of the home.

The elves drove Santa Claus back to Hucklebuckle Toys and then carried him to his room.

"Is he going to be okay?" Mrs. Huckle asked.

Eli shook his head sadly. Things weren't looking good. Santa had been without his crystal for too long.

Paws jumped onto the bed. “Eli, take my crystal off and place it next to Santa’s,” he said.

“Paws, we might not be able to bring you back a second time!” Eddy warned. “You may become a stuffed toy forever.”

“We have no choice,” Paws told Eddy. “Can you imagine a world without Santa Claus?”

Eli took Paws’ crystal and set it beside Santa’s. The glow in Santa’s crystal grew stronger. But it still was not strong enough.

“Can I have some time with Santa alone?” Paws asked.

The others left.

A little while later, Santa's eyes fluttered open. He noticed the two crystals around his own neck. Then he noticed Paws—he was a stuffed toy again.

A moment later, Santa walked out into the main room of the toy store. He was carrying Paws.

The others were happy to see that Santa was feeling better, but they were all concerned for Paws.

"We have to get back to the North Pole," Santa said. "Only the Great Christmas Icicle can save Paws now."

Soon Gus arrived in Santa's sleigh, pulled by the reindeer. Santa and the elves traded heartfelt good-byes with

Quinn, Will, the Huckles, and Gus. Then Santa and the elves took off for the North Pole, flying the sleigh as fast as they could.

Mrs. Claus was relieved when Santa, Eddy, and Eli arrived home safe and sound. Then she saw Paws.

Santa quickly carried Paws into the ice cave. Mrs. Claus, Eddy, and Eli were right behind him. At the Great Christmas Icicle, Santa carefully set Paws down. The Icicle sent a wave of magic to Paws' crystal, but its light was still too faint.

"With Christmas coming so soon, the Icicle doesn't have enough magic to spare," Santa said sadly. "I never thought I'd have such a friend. . . ."

A tear ran down his cheek and dripped onto the floor of the ice cave. There was a pulse of Christmas magic where it fell. The magic spread like a wave and collected at the Icicle.

"What's happening?" Mrs. Claus wondered aloud.

Santa wasn't sure.

First the magic wave changed Paws back into a real puppy. Then he became a medium-sized dog. Finally, the wave changed him into a large, majestic white dog! He was dressed in his own Santa suit and had a big crystal around his neck.

"Paws, you're back!" Santa cried. "But how?"

Mrs. Claus thought she knew. "It was your love for each other," she guessed. "And Christmas magic!"

"What happened to me?" Paws asked.

"You're no longer a pup," Santa told him proudly. "From now on, your name will be Santa Paws!"

In New York, Mr. and Mrs. Huckle took Quinn and Will back to the home. Mrs. Gibson was relieved to see the girls.

"We'll never forget you," Quinn told Mrs. Huckle.

She and Will both hugged Mrs.

Huckle tightly. Mrs. Huckle had loved having the two girls stay, even for a short time. She was going to miss them.

Mrs. Gibson leaned toward Mr. Huckle. "You know, they need a home," she whispered.

Mr. Huckle decided right then and there that he and his wife would adopt both girls.

"That is the greatest Christmas gift I could ever imagine," Mrs. Huckle said happily. And the rest of her new family felt exactly the same way.

On Christmas Eve, Santa and Paws arrived in the Huckles' living room.

The new family woke up.

"The Great Christmas Icicle brought me back. I'm Santa Paws now," he told Quinn and Will.

"We have everything we ever wanted," Will told him.

The Huckle family decided to stay in New York and run the toy store. They also changed their name back to Hucklebuckle.

Quinn and Will weren't the only ones whose lives had changed because of Santa Claus. The other girls at the home were thrilled to have a new, and much nicer, guardian. Now they could have a Christmas tree!

Gus was different, too. He had

realized he liked being nice and telling the truth. He even gave the rest of the money he had collected to the girls at the home.

Then there were the street dogs. They'd hidden away in the elves' mail truck. When they arrived at the North Pole, Eddy decided to make them official elf dogs! The three newcomers were thrilled, and they soon became hard workers.

Santa's close call even affected people who hadn't met him. Many children had watched the news and seen Santa in the hospital. They wrote letters saying that they didn't care about expensive toys and trinkets.

All they wanted was for Santa to be healthy again.

Paws was just glad to be back in the North Pole. He couldn't wait to help Santa Claus begin preparing for next Christmas!

And that was how the legend of Santa Paws started. Although that wasn't really the end of the story. It was only the beginning. . . .

Part Two

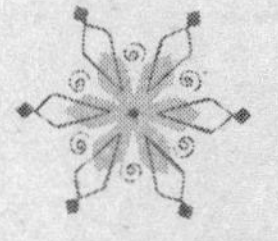

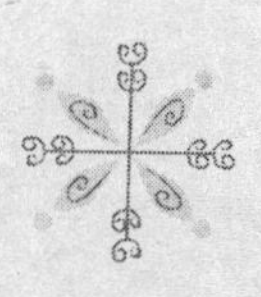

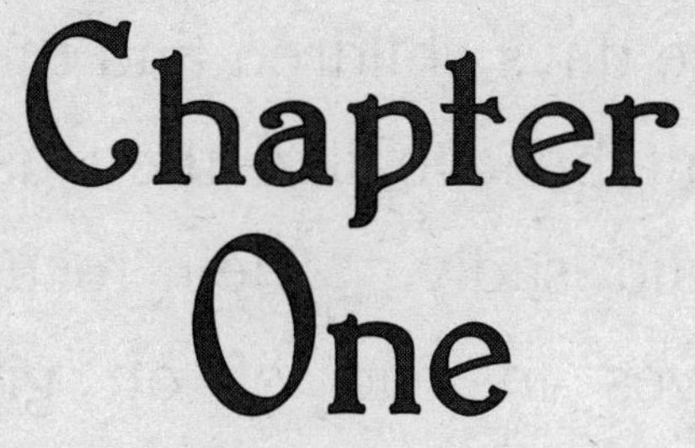

Chapter One

Many years later, the stars shone brightly over the North Pole. Santa Claus entered the ice cave with his best friend, Santa Paws, a large, white dog who wore a red suit similar to Santa's. Water dripped steadily from the Great Christmas Icicle.

Santa Paws looked worried. "If the

Icicle continues to melt at this rate, its magic will vanish," he said.

"These days children and their pups just don't believe like they used to," Santa said sadly. "Their focus is on themselves instead of on giving to others."

"If they don't understand the true meaning of Christmas, the Icicle has no chance," Santa Paws said. "Soon it will be Puppy Paws' responsibility to show the next generation the importance of Christmas spirit."

Santa and Paws looked at each other, concerned. Then they headed back to Santa's workshop.

❄ ❄ ❄

Outside in the snow, Santa's sleigh flew through the air. A fluffy white puppy was seated inside.

"*Wahoo!* Now Dasher, now Dancer!" the pup cried. "*Wahoo!*"

The reindeer brought the sleigh to a stop outside Santa's workshop.

"That was fun!" the puppy cried. "Let's do it again!"

"We're all too tired, Puppy Paws," Comet replied. "Besides, we have to get ready for Christmas Eve. You know, the most important night of the year?"

Puppy Paws made a face. He didn't like doing any work. "Fine! I'll go find some fun on my own."

He jumped out of the sleigh and ran

into Santa's workshop. Inside, everyone was making toys. Eli the head elf and Eddy the elf dog were watching over it all. The elves sang as they worked.

Puppy Paws watched a conveyor belt carry toys from one station to the next. He noticed a switch beside the belt. With a grin, Puppy Paws flipped it from SLOW to FAST.

Suddenly, all the conveyor belts in the workshop began to go faster. The elves couldn't keep up. Unfinished toys flew everywhere!

Puppy Paws giggled as he watched the chaos. Then he looked up and saw Eli frowning at him. Puppy Paws knew he was in trouble.

Chapter Two

"Son, I'm very disappointed in you," Santa Paws said. "You disrupted the workshop and wasted a whole day."

Puppy Paws stood before his father and Santa Claus.

"I just wanted to have some fun," Puppy Paws mumbled. He hung his head, looking sheepish.

"Maybe you should think about how important Christmas is to children and puppies all around the world," Santa Paws said. "It's our responsibility to deliver gifts to all good puppies."

"You mean it's *your* responsibility." Puppy Paws frowned. "I just want to be an ordinary puppy."

Santa Paws did not understand why his son would say that. "You're grounded until further notice. No playing fetch with the elves and no flying with the reindeer!"

"I wish Christmas would just go away!" Puppy Paws cried. He ran out of the room.

Santa Paws glanced over at Santa

Claus. "Do you think I was too strict with him?"

"Maybe a smidgen," Santa replied. "But I'm sure he'll get over it."

Santa Paws nodded, but he was worried. Puppy Paws was the future of Christmas. If he didn't care about the holiday, then who would?

Fernfield, USA, was the home of five playful golden retriever puppies known as the Buddies. The pups all lived with different families. But they liked to get together to have fun.

One December day, they sat outside Fernfield Town Hall watching the townsfolk light the Christmas tree.

One of the puppies, B-Dawg, looked bored. "Why do we even have to come here?" he complained.

Deputy Sniffer, a bloodhound and the Fernfield sheriff's best friend, answered. "It's a Christmas tradition. I've been watching the lighting of the tree since I was a pup like you."

An athletic-looking pup named Budderball looked distracted. "I'm still in the doghouse for eating the Thanksgiving turkey."

"Are you worried you might be on Santa Paws' naughty list?" Deputy Sniffer asked.

"*Pshaw*, Santa Paws is just Dad dressed up in a red-and-white suit!"

B-Dawg scoffed. "They just use it so we behave."

"Let's look at the evidence," his brother, Mudbud, said in agreement. "If the jolly dude actually came down the chimney, wouldn't there be a lot of soot?" Mudbud was an expert on soot—and every other kind of dirt, too.

Their one sister, Rosebud, spoke up. "I'm not really buying the whole Santa Paws thing, either," she said. "But I sure do love all the presents."

"Your material desires are those of the 'wanting mind,'" put in her brother Buddha. "Enough is never enough."

"Getting presents isn't what Christmas is about," Deputy Sniffer agreed. "There are plenty of lonely puppies without families or children to love them."

Just then a beat-up truck cruised past. It had the word DOGCATCHER printed on the side. A grouchy old man was driving.

"Buddies!" Budderball whispered. "It's Mr. Cruge, the dogcatcher!"

None of the puppies liked Stan Cruge. Once the truck had passed, they headed back to their homes.

Later, in another part of town, Mr. Cruge shone a spotlight down an alley. Nothing. After a moment, he drove on.

In the alley, a small puppy named

Tiny breathed a sigh of relief as the truck disappeared. Then he came out of his hiding place and knocked over a garbage can. A half-eaten steak fell out!

Tiny couldn't believe his luck. He grabbed the steak and started to eat hungrily.

WHAM! A net came down around the pup.

"Thought you could run wild in the streets?" Mr. Cruge crowed. "Not on my watch!"

Tiny howled as Mr. Cruge put him into a cage in the back of the truck and slammed the door shut.

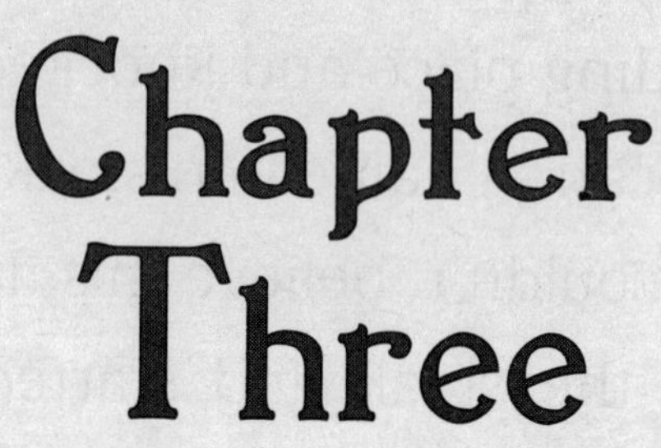

Chapter Three

Santa Claus and Santa Paws sat at a large desk in the workshop. They were going over that Christmas's *nice* and *naughty* lists.

Two massive books were open in front of them. The smaller one was titled *Nice*, and the larger one *Naughty*.

"The *naughty* book gets thicker every

year," Santa remarked. "And we're just on pups!"

Santa Paws was still thinking about his son's behavior earlier that day. "If Puppy Paws doesn't understand the true meaning of Christmas, how can we expect other puppies to?" he asked.

Santa turned a page in the *naughty* book. An image of a golden retriever pup labeled BUDDERBALL appeared. The picture came to life, showing the pup's offense. Santa Claus and Santa Paws watched as Budderball ate his human family's Thanksgiving turkey.

"'Budderball. Offense: gluttony,'" Santa read.

A minute earlier, Puppy Paws had

sneaked into the workshop and watched as his father and Santa Claus went through the *naughty* book. When he saw Budderball fast asleep in the turkey tray, burping happily, Puppy Paws almost laughed aloud. But he didn't want anyone to notice him.

Just then, Eli and Eddy hurried in.

"We've got the mail truck ready for a systems check," Eli announced.

He, Eddy, and Santa hurried out. Santa Paws was right behind them. Puppy Paws came out of hiding for a better look at the *naughty* book.

"'Budderball, one of the five Air Buddies,'" he read aloud. "'He has three brothers—Mudbud, B-Dawg, and

Buddha. A little sis, Rosebud. They live in Fernfield, Washington. Regular, ordinary fun-loving pups.' " Puppy Paws looked up from the book. "They sound perfect!"

He ripped out the page and ran off. He would never get to be a regular dog at the North Pole. So he'd just have to go somewhere else to be normal . . . somewhere like Fernfield.

In the workshop garage, Eli and Eddy were checking the mail truck. They would use it to fly around the world to pick up children's letters to Santa.

"Jingle all the way, Eli," Santa said.

Puppy Paws was watching. "Here I

go," he whispered to himself. "Time to hitch a ride to Fernfield."

Puppy Paws waited until no one was looking, then dashed into the back of the truck. He was carrying the page he'd torn from the *naughty* book in his mouth.

A few hours later, Eli landed the mail truck in front of the Fernfield post office. He got out and hurried inside. Puppy Paws jumped down from the truck and hid behind a bush.

Eli soon returned with a half-full bag of mail. He jumped into the cab and glanced at the truck's power meter.

"Holy Christmas spirit," he said.

"We're almost out of power!"

He quickly started the truck and drove away to finish picking up Santa's mail. Puppy Paws waited until the elf was gone. Then he walked around Fernfield. So this was what being an ordinary pup was like!

In the middle of town, a painter was working on a mural and listening to the radio. As Puppy Paws passed, his collar glowed, and the painter's music changed to a Christmas tune! Surprised, she accidentally splashed paint on her mural.

Puppy Paws didn't notice. He was having too much fun being a regular puppy.

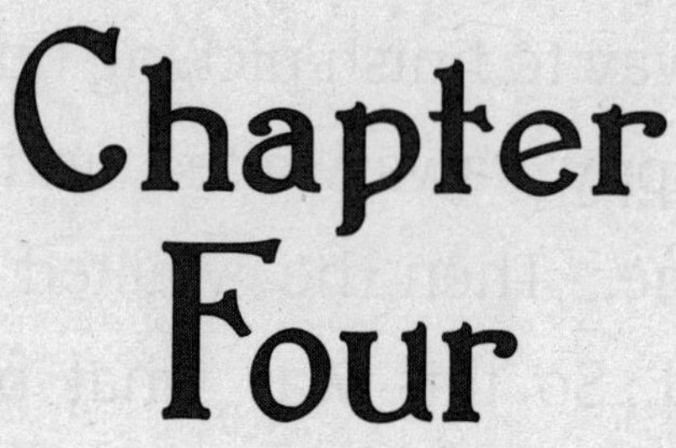

Chapter Four

"I hate to say it," an elf named Ellis said, "but I think the North Pole is starting to melt."

Santa Claus and several elves were examining a box that was wired to power everything in the workshop. Santa shook his head grimly.

"Any thoughts?" he asked.

“Well, sir,” said Eddy, “spirit is down, but there seems to be something else going on. The Icicle is melting faster than we ever thought possible.”

Santa Paws hurried in. “Has anyone seen Puppy Paws?” he asked. “He seems to be missing.”

Santa Claus and the elves shook their heads. Santa Paws was worried. Where could his son be?

When night fell in Fernfield, Puppy Paws was feeling discouraged. He’d been looking for Budderball for hours.

He passed the Christmas tree in front of Town Hall. Next to it was a small stage decorated to look like

Santa's workshop in the North Pole. A bearded man wearing a red suit sat in a chair. A line of children were waiting to tell Santa their Christmas wishes. Puppy Paws thought the man was the real Santa Claus.

"They couldn't have found me already!" he cried.

He bolted across the street toward the stage, running right in front of a truck. The truck screeched to a halt, and the driver narrowed his eyes. It was Mr. Cruge.

Puppy Paws didn't notice the dog-catcher. He was more interested in how Santa had gotten to Fernfield.

When he got closer, Puppy Paws

saw that the man wasn't Santa after all. "*Phew!*" he said. "An imposter."

Then he noticed Mr. Cruge creeping up on him with a net. Puppy Paws dodged him easily. "Hey!" he cried. "What are you doing?"

Mr. Cruge only heard barking. He chased Puppy Paws, but the pup got away.

"People aren't very jolly in Fernfield," Puppy Paws said to himself. "I think it's time to call it a night. I'll have to find Budderball in the morning."

He sneaked into a candy store while its owner was leaving. He curled up in the window display and was soon fast asleep.

❄ ❄ ❄

Back at the North Pole, Santa Paws and everyone else was searching frantically for Puppy Paws. While they were looking, the mail truck returned.

"You're back early," Eddy said to Eli.

"Almost ran out of power," Eli explained.

The other elves went to unload the truck. "Where's all the mail?" an elf named Ellis asked when he noticed there was only half a bag of letters.

"That's all there was," Eli replied.

The other elves traded worried glances. Only half a bag of letters to Santa so close to the holiday? Had the whole world lost its Christmas spirit?

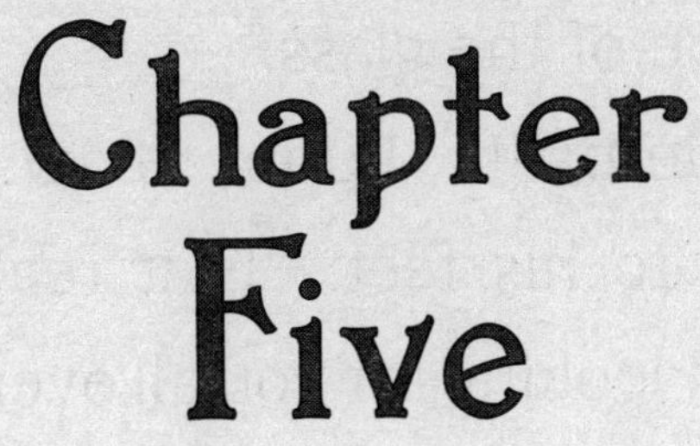

Chapter Five

The next morning, Budderball walked along the street with his owner, Bartleby. The pup, who was almost always hungry, paused to look in the window of the candy shop.

"Gingerbread cookies!" Budderball said, licking his chops.

Puppy Paws woke up. When he

opened his eyes, he recognized the stocky golden retriever pup on the other side of the glass.

"Budderball!" Puppy Paws cried, jumping to his feet. "Is it really you? I've been looking for you all over town!"

He tried to leap at the other pup. But he'd forgotten about the window between them. He bonked his head on the glass.

Outside, Budderball saw the fluffy white pup and thought he was just a puppet in the store's holiday display.

"Wow," Budderball said, "that polar-bear cub sure looks realistic. His mouth even moves."

Then his owner called him, and

Budderball raced off. Puppy Paws couldn't believe it.

"Budderball!" he howled. "Wait!"

By the time Puppy Paws got outside, Budderball was gone.

Puppy Paws hurried down the street. He spotted a bloodhound sleeping on the porch of the sheriff's office.

"Excuse me," he said, waking up Deputy Sniffer. "I'm looking for a pup. His name's Budderball."

"I've known that pup his whole life," Deputy Sniffer said. "He lives at Livingstone Manor."

He told Puppy Paws how to get there. Puppy Paws thanked him and took off.

❄ ❄ ❄

At Livingstone Manor, Bartleby and his dad, James, were decorating the tree while Budderball watched.

"We should lower the candy canes a little," Budderball suggested hungrily. "They're hard to, um . . . see?"

The humans left the room without moving the candy canes. Budderball wondered if he could stretch tall enough to reach one.

Suddenly, a soot-covered white pup tumbled out of the fireplace and crashed right into Budderball! It was Puppy Paws. He'd climbed down the chimney, just like his father. Well, actually, he had fallen down the chimney.

"Budderball!" Puppy Paws cried. "I finally found you! I'm Puppy Paws."

"Where'd you come from?" asked Budderball.

"The North Pole."

"Oh, yeah. I bet you belong to Santa Claus," Budderball said sarcastically.

"Technically, yes," Puppy Paws said. "But Santa Paws is my pop."

Budderball stared at the other pup for a second. Then he cracked up.

"You expect me to believe your dad is Santa Paws?" he exclaimed. "Who put you up to this?"

"No one." Puppy Paws was a little confused. "I was checking the *naughty* list and you looked like fun."

That made Budderball stop laughing. "I'm on the *naughty* list?"

"Don't worry," said Puppy Paws, "you can get onto the *nice* list by doing good deeds for others."

"Like?"

"Well, um . . ." Puppy Paws thought for a second. "Like teaching me how to be an ordinary pup."

Budderball shrugged. "Okay. I'll show you what I like to do."

He led Puppy Paws through the mansion. Soon they were in the house's huge kitchen.

"This is the most magical room in the house," Budderball said.

A bell dinged. The chef took a

pan of cookies out of the oven.

"Is he one of your elves?" Puppy Paws asked.

"You're a real joker, aren't you?" Budderball replied. "That's the chef. He's making cookies. But we can't eat them—they're for Christmas."

As soon as the chef left, Puppy Paws jumped up on the counter.

"Hey, how'd you get up there?" Budderball cried.

Puppy Paws pushed the cookies onto the floor. The crystal on his collar glowed. The treats magically changed from plain sugar cookies into colorful Christmas cookies!

"Wow!" Budderball cried, amazed.

"How'd you do that?" he asked.

Puppy Paws showed off the crystal on his collar. "It's no biggie. Christmas magic is stored in here, so I can do stuff like my dad. But I can't quite control it. Hey, want a cookie?"

"Don't you remember?" Budderball asked him. "I'm trying to get back on the *nice* list!"

He watched as Puppy Paws gobbled up all the cookies. After Puppy Paws finished the last one, he ran outside.

Just then, James walked in and saw Budderball sitting beside the empty cookie sheet.

Busted!

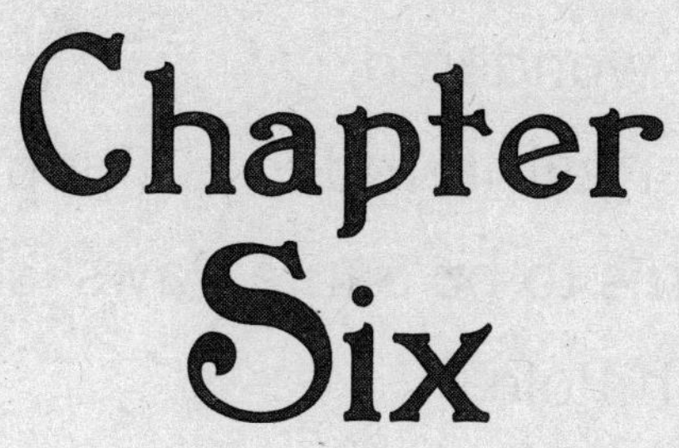

Chapter Six

"Budderball is fashionably late again," Rosebud said.

She was in the park with B-Dawg, Buddha, and Mudbud. All the Buddies were supposed to meet there.

"I hope the dude's not in trouble," Mudbud said.

Finally, they all spotted Budderball.

Puppy Paws was with him.

"Who's the white fluffy dude?" Mudbud wondered.

Budderball introduced Puppy Paws. "He claims to be Santa Paws' son from the North Pole."

"Yo!" B-Dawg exclaimed. "You straight up tripping? We ain't falling for that, dawg!"

"We've grown a little skeptical about Christmas," Buddha admitted.

"You're not alone," Puppy Paws said with a shrug. "No one believes in Christmas spirit anymore. That's why I'm here—to learn how to be an ordinary pup."

"Well, you found the right dawg to

school you," B-Dawg said. "Come on, I'll show you my crib."

He took Puppy Paws to his house. B-Dawg turned on the stereo and showed him some break-dancing moves.

"Let's see you give it a shot, player," B-Dawg said when the song ended.

"Okay," Puppy Paws said. "I'll give it a whirl, player."

He tapped the stereo. His crystal lit up, and the song changed to a mix of hip-hop and Christmas music.

Puppy Paws had some pretty good moves. He ended his dancing with a spin that was so fast he became just a blur. As he spun, he bumped into a table. A vase on top of the table wobbled. . . .

CRASH!

"Did I bust some moves?" Puppy Paws asked when he had stopped spinning.

B-Dawg stared at the broken vase. "You busted something, all right!"

Mudbud was relaxing in a patch of wet dirt when he saw B-Dawg and Puppy Paws coming.

"Yo, dawg," B-Dawg said. "It's your turn to hang with Santa Junior."

"No *problemo*, dude." As B-Dawg stomped off, Mudbud turned to Puppy Paws. "Why's he in such a huff?"

"I dunno, dawg," Puppy Paws said. "He be trippin'."

"*Wowzers*, dude! You don't have to talk like B-Dawg," Mudbud exclaimed.

"Isn't that how ordinary puppies talk?" Puppy Paws asked.

"Dude, only B-Dawg talks like that!" Mudbud said.

Then he showed the other pup how to relax in a mud bath. Puppy Paws dove right in. His fluffy white fur soaked up the wet dirt like a mop.

"Now what, dude?" Puppy Paws asked.

Mudbud shrugged. "Let me show you my sweet pad."

They went inside. The living room

was decorated mostly in white.

"This is the cleanest room in the house," Mudbud said. "Strictly off-limits."

"Dude," Puppy Paws said, wiggling around, "is it normal for mud to feel itchy?"

"No, dude, don't do it!" Mudbud cried.

It was too late. Before the other pup could stop him, Puppy Paws shook himself. Mud flew off him and splattered all over the living room. But a moment later, his crystal glowed and the mud stains changed. Now they looked like brown snowflakes, reindeer, and other Christmas objects. Puppy Paws' coat was pure white again.

"Whoa, how'd you do that?" Mudbud cried.

Just then Mudbud's owner's mom came in. She stared from the sparkling clean Puppy Paws to the still-muddy Mudbud.

Mudbud hung his head. He knew who was going to get blamed for this.

That same day, Mudbud took Puppy Paws to stay with Rosebud at her house.

"So, what sweet stuff are we going to do, dudette?" Puppy Paws asked her.

Rosebud rolled her eyes. "Oh, brother."

She took him inside. Her owner, Alice, had been dressing her in different outfits. The latest was a pretty pink number, but Puppy Paws didn't think it looked very festive. When Alice left the room, his crystal glowed, and suddenly Rosebud was dressed in a green-and-red elf suit!

"*Aaaaaaah!*" Rosebud cried in horror. The whole outfit was a crime against fashion! Rosebud glared at Puppy Paws, but he didn't understand what he had done wrong.

Later, Buddha was meditating in the Zen garden behind his owner's house. *"Om . . ."* Buddha chanted as he sat in front of his Buddha statue. *"Om . . ."*

Puppy Paws bounded in.

"Rosebud sent me," he announced. "She was, like, totally freaking out about her Christmas makeover."

"A clear mind is developed through meditation," Buddha told Puppy Paws calmly. He invited him to join in.

Puppy Paws tried to meditate. But he accidentally turned the Buddha statue into a snowman and the Zen garden into a Christmas display. Even Buddha, who hardly ever became upset, couldn't stay calm about something like that.

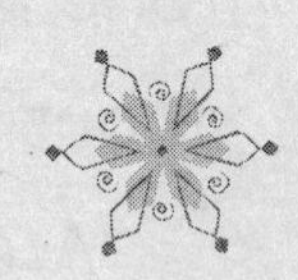

Chapter Seven

Across town, a man named Bob had just entered one of the most un-Christmas-like places in Fernfield: the dog pound. It was a damp, dark, rundown place. Bob's son, Mikey, was sick and wanted a puppy for Christmas. Bob wanted to make his son's wish come true.

Mr. Cruge led him to a row of cages in the back. In the last cage was a group of puppies. The littlest one was named Tiny. Bob stared at him. The puppy looked so small and in need of love.

"This is the one," he said as Tiny licked his hand. "He's perfect."

"That one's three hundred dollars," Mr. Cruge said.

"I thought the puppies were free for adoption," Bob said, confused. "We'll give him a loving home." He checked his pockets. "I have fifty dollars."

But Mr. Cruge wouldn't budge on the price. Bob would have no choice but to leave without Tiny.

"If you can find it in your heart . . ."

Bob said sadly, pulling out a piece of paper. It was Mikey's note to Santa, asking for a puppy. He left it with Mr. Cruge, then headed home.

The next day, Mudbud, Rosebud, Budderball, and B-Dawg gathered at the park.

"I sent Puppy Paws to Buddha's," Rosebud told the others. "I thought he might be the only one with the patience to handle him."

Finally Buddha and Puppy Paws arrived. Buddha was hanging his head in shame.

"So how'd it go?" Rosebud asked.

"I lost it," Buddha admitted. "My

temper." He glared at Puppy Paws.

Suddenly Rosebud had an idea. "I know something that ordinary puppies do," she said. "Play hide-and-seek!"

The others caught on quickly. They told Puppy Paws to close his eyes and count down from twelve.

That sounded like fun to Puppy Paws! He closed his eyes.

"Twelve drummers drumming . . ." he began. "Eleven pipers piping . . ."

He kept counting down while the Buddies took off. They met up again nearby. That gave them a chance to talk about what to do with Puppy Paws. They were all upset that he'd gotten them in trouble.

Each pup took turns complaining about what Puppy Paws had done. They didn't notice that Puppy Paws had finished counting and come to find them. He had heard every word!

"I was just trying to be like them," he whispered sadly.

He sneaked away again, but this time he didn't care where he was headed.

Meanwhile, the Buddies had already started to feel bad about what they'd just said.

"Puppy Paws isn't responsible for me losing my center," Buddha said. "To find faults in him, we're really just finding faults in ourselves."

Mudbud nodded. "He was only trying to fit in."

Puppy Paws was already too far away to hear them, though. He was so upset that he didn't notice Mr. Cruge sneaking up on him.

Whoosh! The dogcatcher's net swept him up.

Before he knew it, Puppy Paws was at the pound. Mr. Cruge took off Paws' collar, then tossed him into the cage with the rest of the pups. Puppy Paws looked at Tiny and the others.

"What's with that guy?" Puppy Paws asked. He nodded his head in the direction Mr. Cruge had gone. "Did he get coal in his stocking or something?"

"He lost his Christmas spirit," replied Tiny.

"No one cares about Christmas anymore," Puppy Paws scoffed.

"We do," said Tiny. "The hope for a Christmas miracle is all we have."

Puppy Paws felt ashamed when he realized that Tiny really *did* believe in the spirit of the holiday. Puppy Paws felt bad that he had made fun of it—after all, he knew better than anyone that Christmas magic really existed.

"We *need* a Christmas miracle," Tiny continued. He looked around at the other puppies in the straw-lined cage. They nodded.

"I had no idea," Puppy Paws said

softly. These pups were in a bad place, but they hadn't given up hope. If they could still believe, then he should, too.

A little while later, all the puppies curled up together to go to sleep. Just before he drifted off, Puppy Paws hoped that he hadn't made too big a mess of things back at the North Pole. He had to get out of the pound and go home to set things right. But was it too late?

Chapter Eight

Santa Claus and Santa Paws were in the ice cave at the North Pole.

"The Christmas Icicle is almost gone," Santa Paws said, staring at what was left of the Icicle. "When Puppy Paws left, it started melting even faster. If we don't find him, Christmas as we know it will be lost forever!"

He and Santa went back to the workshop. They learned that Eli had just found something in the back of the mail truck—Puppy Paws' suit and the page he'd torn from the *naughty* book!

Santa Paws and Santa Claus were starting to feel weaker and weaker as the Icicle dripped away. They needed the elves to help get Puppy Paws back.

Eli and Eddy were ready. "We'll be back quicker than you can say Candy Cane Lane!" Eddy promised.

The elf and elf dog took off for Fernfield in Santa's mail truck.

"We made it," Eli said as the truck rolled to a stop in front of Fernfield

Town Hall. "I have no idea how we're going to get back, though. The tank is completely out of magic."

Eddy hopped out of the truck. "I'll try to find Puppy Paws," he said.

Eli nodded. "I'll see what I can do about the truck."

As Eddy raced off, the elf stared at the truck, worried. Even if they found Puppy Paws, how were they supposed to get him back to the North Pole without any magical power?

The Buddies felt terrible about losing Puppy Paws. They met up again at the park later that day. Soon everyone was there except Budderball.

"Being fashionably late is one thing, but this is way out of style," Rosebud complained.

Then Mudbud spotted Budderball heading toward them. "Dude," he said, "am I hallucinating, or is Budderball running with an elf?"

Budderball and Eddy rushed up.

"Sorry I'm late," Budderball said. "This is Eddy. He claims to be Santa Paws' head elf."

"We need your help," Eddy said. "Christmas is in great danger. We need to get Puppy Paws back to the North Pole!"

"There's one obstacle," Buddha said. "Puppy Paws has disappeared."

Just then, Mudbud spotted the dogcatcher's truck. "Quick, hide!" he cried. "It's Cruge!"

The puppies all hid in the bushes.

"Do you think Puppy Paws might be in the pound?" Rosebud wondered aloud, worried.

They all traded looks. Mr. Cruge always snatched up any dog he could. What if he'd snagged Puppy Paws?

The Buddies all took off running toward the dog pound, with Eddy right behind them.

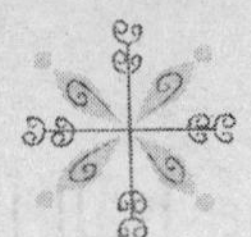

Chapter Nine

"Okay, you know the plan," Rosebud whispered, once they were inside the pound. "Budderball, you're on lookout. Mudbud and B-Dawg, you find the key. Buddha, Eddy, and I will find Puppy Paws. Got it?"

The others nodded.

Eddy, Buddha, and Rosebud headed

down the hall lined with cages.

"Puppy Paws?" Eddy called softly. "Are you in here?"

"Eddy, is that you?" a voice called.

Eddy and the others rushed to a cage in the back.

"The Christmas Icicle is all but melted now," Eddy told Puppy Paws. "Santa Claus and Santa Paws need you back!"

"Your dad is Santa Paws?" Tiny asked. "There isn't going to be a Christmas?"

"I won't let that happen, Tiny," Puppy Paws said. "You pups taught me the true meaning of Christmas spirit. It's not about presents at all. It's about things you can't wrap in a box or tie with a bow." He paused. "Find my collar so we can get out of here!"

Buddha and Budderball ran to the office where they found Mudbud and B-Dawg. It didn't take long for them to find Puppy Paws' collar.

Budderball slipped the collar under the cage door. Puppy Paws put it on. The crystal lit up, and the cage opened.

"I can't thank you guys enough!" Puppy Paws told the Buddies.

"That's what friends do," Budderball said. "Help each other out of a jam."

They had all forgotten that Budderball was supposed to be standing watch. Suddenly Mr. Cruge appeared. He had the dogs cornered!

"You guys go," Eddy told the Buddies

and Puppy Paws. "I'll take care of him."

"We'll help," Tiny piped up. He and the other puppies stepped forward.

"You'd be willing to do that?" Puppy Paws asked. He knew that Tiny was giving up his own chance to escape.

"It's us or saving Christmas, right?" Tiny said bravely.

"Go!" Eddy ordered Puppy Paws. "Eli's waiting in front of Town Hall."

Tiny and the other puppies charged at Mr. Cruge. They jumped up on him, barking and distracting him. When they licked his face, he suddenly started laughing. "I'm ticklish!" he cried.

In the confusion, Puppy Paws and the Buddies ran off.

❄ ❄ ❄

"Eli, wake up!" Puppy Paws cried. He had spotted Eli in a sleigh that was part of the Town Hall holiday display. "We've got to get back to the North Pole!"

"The truck doesn't have enough power," Eli said. "I've been trying to figure out how to get this sleigh to work, but . . ." He paused, staring at Puppy Paws' collar. "Your collar might have enough magic to make this thing fly."

"We need reindeer."

"There are no reindeer in Fernfield," Budderball told Puppy Paws.

Rosebud smiled. She had an idea about how to get the sleigh back to the North Pole.

Chapter Ten

Back at the pound, Mr. Cruge finished locking Tiny and the others back in their cage. “For that little stunt, there will be no dinner,” he growled at the pups.

“We know all about you at the North Pole,” a voice said.

“Who said that?” Mr. Cruge demanded.

Then he realized the voice was

coming from inside Eddy's cage.

"You didn't get a puppy when you were a boy," Eddy said. "It made you hate Christmas."

Eddy was using the crystal on his collar so Mr. Cruge could understand him. He felt sorry for the dogcatcher and hoped he could make Christmas magical for him again.

"Are you talking to me?" Mr. Cruge exclaimed.

"The best way to heal your broken heart is to give to those in need," Eddy told him. "It's time to let Christmas back in your heart."

His crystal glowed, and he walked through the bars out of the cage.

"I'd love to stay for eggnog," Eddy said. "But I have to get back to the North Pole and help save Christmas."

He dashed out of the pound as Mr. Cruge stared after him in amazement.

The Buddies were now hitched to the sleigh, with B-Dawg in the lead.

"Okay, you're all set," Eli told them. "We only have one shot at this, so it's important you believe you can fly—without a shadow of a doubt."

"Ready, Buddies?" Puppy Paws called from inside the sleigh.

"That's *rein*-dogs to you, bro!" Mudbud called back.

"Next stop, the North Pole!"

Puppy Paws' crystal began to glow. The Buddies started to pull. At first the sleigh just slid along the grass.

Then it started to fly!

"Whoa, I'm flying!" B-Dawg cried.

"I'm afraid of heights!" Budderball squeezed his eyes shut. "By the way, does anyone actually know how to get to the North Pole?"

"Just follow the North Star."

Puppy Paws was sure his new friends would do their best to help him get home. Would they arrive in time?

A short while later, the sleigh landed in the North Pole. The Buddies had pulled it safely the entire way.

"Dad!" Puppy Paws shouted as he burst into Santa's workshop.

"Son!" Santa Paws cried.

"I'm so sorry for not believing," Puppy Paws said, apologizing. "I just didn't understand how important Christmas was."

"And I'm sorry I was hard on you," his dad said. "I should have trusted you to come to that realization by yourself."

"Well, it took the help of a few friends." Puppy Paws smiled at the Buddies, who had followed him in.

Santa Paws smiled, too. "Nice to see you again, Buddies. Any more turkey infractions, Budderball?"

"No, Mr. Paws," Budderball said. "I

haven't even sneaked a cookie."

"We'll have to see about getting you off Santa's *naughty* list," Santa Paws promised. "And thank you all for coming. We're very busy here, and it's going to take all the help we can get to make Christmas happen."

The Buddies were ready to pitch in. They promised to help the elves and elf dogs finish the toys for the world's children and puppies.

"Ho, ho, ho!" Santa Claus chuckled as he walked in. "We are back in business!"

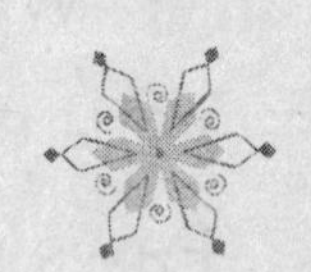

Chapter Eleven

It was Christmas Eve. The Icicle was gaining strength every minute now that Puppy Paws believed in the magic of Christmas. Everyone was relieved. But as the reindeer lined up in front of Santa's sleigh, they still seemed weak.

"We're ready for the test flight," Comet told Santa.

"Okay, everyone, let's cross our fingers and paws," Santa said.

The reindeer tried and tried, but they couldn't make the sleigh budge. They collapsed on the ground, exhausted.

"Comet! Donner! Blitzen!" Santa cried. "Are you okay?"

"Sorry, Santa," Comet said. "We still don't seem to have enough strength to fly even the empty sleigh."

"The Christmas Icicle is growing," Santa Paws said. "But not fast enough."

"The Buddies and I flew that small sleigh to the North Pole with just the little magic that was left in my crystal," Puppy Paws said. "Maybe we can do it again!"

The Buddies nodded eagerly. They would be happy to help Santa deliver the toys.

Soon the Buddies were hitched to the smaller sleigh.

"Prepare for departure," Eli told them.

"Good luck, son," Santa Paws said. "Stay focused. Tonight is the most important night of the year."

"All good children and puppies are counting on you," Santa Claus added.

Puppy Paws hopped into the sleigh. "No matter what happens tonight, I want to thank you, Buddies," he said. "You're the best friends I've ever had."

"We should thank *you*," Rosebud replied. "We'd stopped believing in

Christmas until we met you."

All together, the Buddies started to run. A moment later, they were flying! Soon the small sleigh was high in the air over the North Pole, heading south.

In Fernfield, most townspeople were happy and waiting for Christmas to arrive. But at a few houses, holiday spirit was overcome by worry.

At Mudbud's house, Pete stared at the Christmas tree. It just wasn't the same without his puppy around. Where was he?

B-Dawg's owner was wondering the same thing. So were Buddha's, Rosebud's, and Budderball's owners.

None of them had any idea what had happened to their dogs. All they could do was ask Santa to grant one important Christmas wish—to send their pups safely home.

After his encounter with Eddy, Mr. Cruge had rediscovered his Christmas spirit. He'd offered all the dogs in the pound free to good homes. All were quickly adopted . . . except for one.

Mr. Cruge picked up Tiny and tucked him into his coat. Then he headed out into the snowy night.

When he reached Mikey's house, he saw the sick little boy and his parents through the window. They were sitting in front of a burning fireplace, sipping hot cocoa.

"Merry Christmas," Mr. Cruge said to Tiny, taking him out of his coat. "I think you're going to make that boy very happy."

He put Tiny down on the stoop and rang the doorbell. Then he hurried away.

A moment later, Mikey opened the door. When he saw Tiny on the porch, he could hardly believe his eyes.

"Mom, Dad!" he cried. "Look what Santa brought me!"

He hugged Tiny, and the pup happily licked Mikey's face. It was the most perfect Christmas either of them could have imagined!

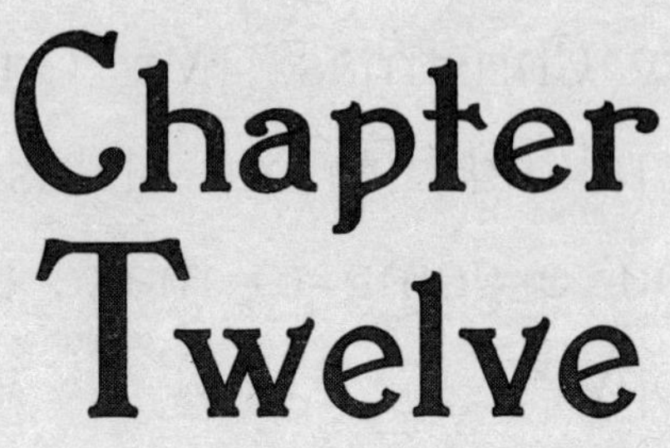

Chapter Twelve

Puppy Paws and the Buddies flew through the sky, pulling the sleigh. They delivered gifts all over the world and had the time of their lives! Puppy Paws couldn't have been happier. He felt as if he were spreading Christmas spirit across the globe.

Finally, Puppy Paws and the Buddies

returned to Fernfield. They safely landed the sleigh in the town square.

"That's it, Buddies," Puppy Paws said. "Our last delivery. We did it!"

"Uh, dude?" Mudbud said. "How are you going to get home with no one to fly your sleigh?"

"Ho, ho, ho!" A jolly laugh rang out.

It was Santa Claus! The Icicle was finally back to full strength, and so were the reindeer. They'd brought Santa Claus and Santa Paws to pick up Puppy Paws.

"Great work, pups!" Santa said. "The North Pole is back in business." Then he gave the Buddies their very own Santa hats.

"Merry Christmas, Buddies," Santa Paws said. Then he turned to his son. "And one more thing . . ."

Santa Paws' crystal glowed. A smaller version of his red suit suddenly appeared on Puppy Paws.

"You earned this, son," Santa Paws said proudly.

Then it was time for Puppy Paws to say good-bye to the Buddies. He was really going to miss them. But he knew he'd see them next Christmas.

"Now, Buddies," Santa said, "you'd better get home to your kids."

The Buddies waved as Santa Claus, Santa Paws, Puppy Paws, and the sleigh pulled by reindeer disappeared into the night sky. Then the Buddies all ran home to make their owners' Christmas wishes come true.

Heading back to the North Pole, Puppy Paws proudly looked down at his new red suit. He'd helped to save the holiday after all, and he'd made the best friends a pup could ask for—the Buddies! It had been his most magical Christmas ever.